SONNY SAYS

Mine!

CARYL HART

illustrated by **ZACHARIAH OHORA**

BLOOMSBURY
CHILDREN'S BOOKS

NEW YORK LONDON OXFORD NEW DELHI SYDNEY

It's a lovely day.

Sonny and his friends are
having fun in the playground when . . .

Ooh!

Sonny finds a thing.

Sonny says,

SO soft. SO cute. SO cuddly.
I'll call you **Bun-Bun**!

Here comes Meemo. Meemo gives Bun-Bun a sniff.
Sonny says,

Mine!

Sonny LOVES playing with Bun-Bun.

Sonny says,

Eat up,
Bun-Bun!

and

Wheee!

Sonny says,

Story time!

and

Night night,
Bun-Bun!

He forgets all about playing with his friends until . . .

Along come Honey and Boo.
Oh dear! Boo is crying.

Honey looks all around . . .

Sonny says,

No!

Sonny looks at
Bun-Bun.

Meemo looks at
Bun-Bun.

Sonny says,

Mine!

He LOVES Bun-Bun
SO much.

Sonny puts Bun-Bun in a safe place.

Sonny says,

Stay there, Bun-Bun!

Then he goes to
find his friends.

But Boo doesn't
want to play.

She just wants Suki.

Sonny says,

Chocolate cake?

But Boo is too sad to eat.

And now Sonny feels sad too.

What will he do?

Will Sonny do the right thing?

Will he?

Will he?

Suki!

Sonny says,